Groundwood Books / House of Anansi Press
groundwoodbooks.com

With the participation of the Government of Canada
Avec la participation du gouvernement du Canada | Canadä

Library and Archives Canada Cataloguing in Publication
Feder, Sandra V., author
The moon inside / written by Sandra V. Feder ; illustrated by Aimée Sicuro.
Issued in print and electronic formats.
ISBN 978-1-55498-823-5 (bound).
— ISBN 978-1-55498-824-2 (pdf)
I. Sicuro, Aimée, illustrator II. Title.
PZ7.F334Mo 2016   j813'.6   C2015-903786-7
C2015-903787-5

The illustrations were done in mixed media, gouache and ink and edited digitally.
Design by Michael Solomon
Printed and bound in Malaysia

For Ellie, Abby and Rachel,
who shine so beautifully and brightly.
SVF

For Yukiko and MJ, thank you for
showing me how to be brave
in the dark.
AS

the moon inside

Sandra V. Feder

Pictures by
Aimée Sicuro

GROUNDWOOD BOOKS
HOUSE OF ANANSI PRESS
TORONTO   BERKELEY

EVERY NIGHT, when the dark entered the house, traveling slowly down the walls and over the floors, Ella grew afraid.

She would take her mother's hand and lead her from room to room. In each room, Ella turned on lights to make the dark go away.

One evening, when dusk was just beginning
to settle over the house, Ella reached again for
her mother's hand.

"The sun is leaving now," Ella said, looking out the window.

"Yes," said Mother. "The sun belongs to the daytime."

"The sun makes me happy. Yellow is
my favorite color," Ella said.
"But now it's almost nighttime again."

Mother opened the door and stepped outside.
"Do you see anything in the night sky?" she asked.

"The moon," Ella said, spotting it low on the horizon.

She watched.
Fireflies danced over the lawn.
"They're glowing," she said, pointing.
"Like the moon."

She listened.
"It's quiet," she said.
She heard the crickets chirp and
the wind in the trees.

Ella and her mother sat on the porch.
They listened some more to the sounds
of the night.
  "I like it here," Ella said.
  "Me, too," said Mother.

Before they went back into the house,
Ella looked up at the golden moon.
"It's my favorite color — only quieter,"
she said.

That night she turned on fewer
lights in the house.
　　She wanted to make sure she could
see the moon in the night sky.

As Ella lay in bed, she knew that she would awake to the bright sun and a brand-new day.

But right now, she was happy that the night belonged to the moon, quietly glowing through her bedroom window.